SIRENS

BOOK 4 - THE EDEN EAST NOVELS

SACHA BLACK

To you, the wonderful readers who followed Eden on this journey. I hope you enjoy the Easter egg.

ONE

What happens to the dead's memories?

I died.

Or a part of me died, and I got stuck in Obex. I wandered through this derelict, balance-forsaken shit hole, when I found you. So I picked you up and here we are.

I've been here a week already. I'm sitting in a dingy bar that I now own—after a short but violent fight, but that's another story. I'm on a balcony that separates the bar from a warehouse that we're turning into a fight club. Which also isn't important.

I'm not very good at this. Let me start again...

I need you—an outlet just for me, something that isn't my essence or skin and bone harboring all my festering memories—and all the memories I've stolen.

Which is why, and I don't want you to take this personally, but when I leave—and I *will* leave—you're staying. This, me and you, it's a temporary thing. Something to stop any demonic madness from creeping in. I have a feeling that if I don't get some of these memories out of my head, they're going to eat me up down here. This place is crawling with all things misery and decay. I've made too many mistakes in life, I could easily fall prey to demonism.

My memories are all I have left of her, of home. I've lost count of the number of times I've spun up her memory ball. My memories too—in fact, any of the memories I've stolen over the years. But all they do is replay the fuckups I've made over and over again.

So here I am, pouring out my mistakes for you to store instead. You're the perfect listener. You won't answer back.

You won't judge, will you?

This way I can figure out what went wrong. And when I'm done here, when Rozalyn has her army, and I leave you behind...

I hope you'll keep my secrets.

TWO

'There are three eternals: Balance, the soul and love.'

Teachings of The First Fallon

Memories from 2007

I was twelve when both my parents died. They'd died less than two months apart. Kato was only ten. Kale—Dad—went first. Mom spiraled after that, she couldn't accept he was gone, wouldn't allow his Dusting. Then, just as suddenly, she vanished, too.

Supposedly, my dad died in a training accident on Earth. He left a few days before. He kissed the pair of us like everything was normal. Ruffled Kato's constantly messy hair and placed a kiss on my forehead.

"Be strong," he said and then he went. I wondered for a long time after his death whether subconsciously he knew he was going to die.

I know now that was a lie. Another hushed-up secret like so many other things surrounding The First Fallon.

I've been spending time with Bellamy, Hermia's husband. He told me what had happened. Kale had gone hunting for a Soul Scythe on Earth. The Libra Legion wanted to use it to kill The First Fallon. He died for it. Touched the blade without gloves and the serrated edge nicked his finger and the fucking knife poisoned him. The only reason Bellamy knows is because he found Kale wandering the streets of Obex searching for the Soul Sanctuary and saved him from a rather nasty fear demon.

I didn't Inherit the extra power at that point though. And that's the weirdest part. For an Inheritance, both parents have to die simultaneously. It was some weird magic my mother did in order to make me Inherit.

I recall those early nights after Dad died. One night in particular, I rolled over and rubbed the nightmares away. I pulled the covers tight under my chin. A beam of white light showered our room with an eerie, raw sensation. The mansion was freezing. Like losing Father had left a hole in the house as well as our family. I glanced at Kato—we shared a room for a while after Dad passed. Soft snuffles came from under the blond locks covering his face. His eyes were still puffy from crying himself to sleep. He was always closer to Father than I was. Muffled sobs drifted from across the hall. Mom. She was crying again, too. I slid out of bed and padded on tiptoes to Mom's door. I hovered, my hands on the frame, wondering if I should go to her. Up to that point, she hadn't cried in front of us. Not even as Israel arrived at our door wearing a grim look. She slid down the door frame, clutched her knees before Israel even opened his mouth.

She knew.

Her reaction, the quiet tearing of her chest, which pummeled my essence so hard and fast I stumbled back, told me everything. That was how I found out my father had died. Not from Israel's words, but from my mother's reaction.

I pushed Kato behind me so he didn't get hit by her emotions. So he could be told in a gentler way.

Waves of despair hit me in the stomach, the chest. They ploughed into my thighs and head. Cold and crushing. Bitter tastes like ice and fermented lemon. The waves throbbed and pelted me again and again. Waves of frozen aches followed by wrenching emptiness. That was the day I learned to hate hopelessness. As she inhaled and struggled to control her emotions. Israel glanced at me, his brows knitted in sympathy.

"Come on, Kato," I said, and wheeled him out of the foyer.

Mom might've thought she'd protected us, saving her tears until we were asleep. But her pain was too big, too consuming. She spent all day silent, muted from the effort of suppressing her feelings. But then she'd break the dam she'd built and the crushing flood of emotion would wake me night after night, thrashing against my essence. I'd slide down the wall outside her bedroom and listen to the sobs until her rhythmic moans sent me back to sleep.

That night, I peered into her room. She was lying on a sofa facing the end of her four-poster bed. The dark wood posts carved into sculptures of famous Siren ancestors, Karva, the first Siren, Tilas, Silvian, and Tortilinos her multiple great grandfather.

The bed's maroon drapes were tied back, revealing the untouched bed. The covers were neat, Father's nightclothes were still strewn across his side of the bed in the same place they were yesterday, and the day before that. There was an almost imperceptible film of dust in the room. As if Mom pressed pause on their bedroom the moment he died and everything was exactly where he left it a couple of weeks ago.

But he wasn't coming back, and she couldn't live in one paused moment. This wasn't a photograph. We needed her. I needed her. I glanced back at our room. Kato was in the same position, with the same swollen lids.

Echoes of his night cries still haunt me. I used to hold him in my arms the best I could until he slept. I did what she should have. Her arms should have been around both of us. But then, I guess she never was there for us. She was more concerned with her own grief than her children's.

She was on the sofa facing the bed, clutching a top of Father's. In her other hand was a memory ball.

I crouched down and leaned against the wall just outside her room so she couldn't see me. For a while, I sat there and watched her encased in pain. Fat tears rolled down her tanned cheeks. They gripped her entire body, shuddering her figure like the strangled cry of a dying animal. I examined the way her shoulders convulsed with every moan, the way her mouth parted and juddered as guttural sobs escaped.

I should have felt sorry for her. I should have clung to her and told her it was going to be okay. That I was sorry he'd left us, but we'd survive. But I didn't because I didn't believe we would. She was breaking, piece by piece, night by night, and I watched it happen.

Now I realize, she should have been in a coma, or dead shortly after. But she survived. Perhaps her Binding wasn't right, or maybe she is stronger than I gave her credit for. Back then, the only thing I wanted to do was trash her room and burn the pause button she'd trapped us and the house in. Hot, frothing rage burrowed its way into my chest and nestled itself beside my heart. She was abandoning us. She was a Siren queen, and she was allowing herself to be consumed by pain. It was a travesty and embarrassment. I knew that and I was only twelve. She should have known better, been able to deal with the loss better. But then who am I to judge? I'm sitting here in Obex, torturing myself and barely coping with the prospect of the century of time I'll have to wait before my Balancer returns to me.

Eventually, Mom's sobs turned to soft breaths and then snuffled snores. Her hand fell slack and Father's top fluttered to the floor.

I stayed for a while, until the sky lightened, and the first rays of dawn painted her room in golden light. The ball of memories in her palm dissolved into nothingness and sleep took her into a few moments of respite.

Staring at her, I realized I was ashamed. Of what she'd done, of how she was behaving, and of how she was abandoning us. So I took some of her pain away. I knew it was dangerous. There were Balancers who got addicted to pain removal. But something about the way her sadness rolled through my essence and power told me it wasn't a normal Balancer loss. She was detached from it. It's only now as I write this that I realize her Binding and the loss of her Balancer felt the same as when I lost Eve. I suspect my mother's Binding was a misbind—she shouldn't have been with Kale. She was fated to another.

Perhaps that's why she never became addicted, that and the fact she had no idea I was taking it. Little by little, night after night, I took tiny pieces of hurt. Small enough, she didn't notice. I didn't do it for her. I did it for Kato because he needed his mother's arms around him while he grieved.

He needed the soft whisper of her calming voice, telling him we would be fine.

I snuck through the door and padded as quiet as I could to the sofa. Her hand hung off the side, so I placed my index finger beneath it, closed my eyes, and took a breath. Then I drew a few tiny pieces of her pain out and let them drift into the air and dissolve into nothingness.

Her shoulders relaxed, her face a little softer and the lines in her brow a little smoother.

When she woke the next morning, she left her bedroom for the first time since he'd died and made us both breakfast. Kato even perked up, seeing her out of her room.

I continued every night until eventually, she, too, vanished from our lives.

THREE

'Where there is love, there is no darkness.'

Burundian

Memories from 2010

I should have started at the beginning. That's where stories are meant to start.

I met Eden when I was six, and she was four. I didn't understand love or fate then. All I knew was that I really wanted to be her friend. I liked the way her curls bounced around her head like coiled springs. Her eyes were still brown then, but threaded through both her irises was a flash of the lilac they'd become.

She was with Beatrice when they walked into one of the Council's meetings. Our parents were busy dealing with a minor Alteritus outbreak, or some other Council nonsense.

Kato and I, Beatrice, Victor and Eden, were all bundled into a room with Nivvy Pushton, the Council secretary, who looked more than put out that they'd allocated her babysitting duty.

Eden inched toward me. I was a couple of years ahead of her at school, so she knew Kato better than me at that point. But as Kato went off to play with Beatrice and Victor, Eden made her way over. My heart leaped into my mouth and my eyes lit up as she joined me. I wanted to play with her desperately, but didn't know how to ask.

"Want to play catch the essence?" she said, her smile wide.

I grinned back and threw a memory ball in the air and tapped her shoulder tagging her "it."

But that's not really what I want to write about. Today, I have to tell you about the biggest betrayal in my life.

Before I died, Eden told me Lani—my mother—was still alive. I don't know whether I believe her. It's not like I can check the Soul Sanctuary. And if both my parents are dead, it means they've likely moved on to the next life and won't be in the Soul Sanctuary, anyway. But what reason would Eden have to lie? My Inheritance is a mystery as it is. You're not meant to Inherit additional powers unless both of your parents die simultaneously. Mine didn't. So who's to say Mom didn't do something insane like strip herself of her powers instead of dying?

My Inheritance wasn't as public as Eden's. The night before it happened, Mom had been behaving oddly. She'd hurried around the house, tidying and cleaning and holding objects. I'd asked her what was wrong, but she'd just looked at me with watery eyes and squeezed my hand. She was suppressing because instead of my essence seeking her emotions, there was a hollow void. That night, she kissed both of us goodnight and held me so tight I thought I'd suffocate.

I'm not sure if it was the Inheritance or the rage that made me forget exactly what she'd said to me as she pecked my forehead and squeezed me, but the memory has been lost to time's shadows.

I'd woken a few hours later and peered out the window. It was midnight; the sky wiped with coal black and diamond studs. I'd poked my head around into her bedroom. She was sitting in the middle of the floor, her back to me, both hands on her knees as she weaved her essence through the air like silken threads. One of her hands stroked it and twirled her fingers through it. Then she closed her fist, and it all vanished, so I ran to my room before she caught me out of bed.

That was the last time I saw her.

In the morning, she'd gone. She didn't even say goodbye. I think that's what hurt the most. If Eden is right and Lani is alive, I could have forgiven her if she'd just explained. Told me what she had to do and why she had to go. Instead, she took the coward's route and just vanished as if she ceased to exist. One moment, our healing lives were on track to recover from the loss of my father and the next, our entire world was broken apart.

When I realized I was alone with Kato in the mansion, I called for Magnus.

He lived on the mansion grounds, albeit in another building. He slammed open the front door, his beard and dreadlocks more unkempt than usual. His eyes swollen with exhaustion, though the blue of his irises shone bright against his dark skin.

"Mother's gone," I said, tremors already edging into my voice. "Did you take her somewhere?"

There was a millisecond beat before he responded. Enough for a tremble to flicker through his expression.

"No."

"She's gone. We should call someone."

Magnus wiped his hand over his face and beard and then pulled out his CogTracker.

Of course, they commissioned Hermia to track Mom, but it was determined pretty quickly that Lani wasn't in Trutinor. All Hermia had to do was track her essence. To this day, Lani is the only failure I've ever known Hermia to have. That's why she was convinced Lani was dead.

By the afternoon, Israel, Arden, Magnus and Hermia had made their way to my living room. All of them wearing grave expressions. Kato was oblivious to what was going on. He sat on the floor playing with cogs and bits of wiring, trying to build some CogBot. I hadn't told him Mom was missing. That came later. I couldn't shatter his world until I knew for sure she was dead.

Arden carried a tray of drinks and some food for us. Hermia strolled in behind him, carrying two bottles of whisky and a stack of tumblers. Both of them halted halfway across the room. Their lips parted, eyes widened.

Something hit me from behind and I stumbled to my knees and slammed into the coffee table.

Pieces of cog and electrical wiring scattered to the floor. Kato glared at me and stood up, hands on his hips.

"Oi," he snapped and then fell silent.

It was Magnus who moved next. Everyone else was motionless, still gawping at me.

Magnus scruffed Kato and pulled him to safety, flinging the table aside in one swift motion.

Whatever had slammed into me hit me again, this time in my thigh. The impact was so violent I collapsed on the floor. A maroon threadlike bolt embedded itself in my trousers, pierced right through the fabric and latched onto my skin.

I don't remember screaming. But I remember Kato's expression. His face dropped. His hands shot to his ears, tears welled in his eyes. He leaned into Magnus, who picked him up and held him tight.

More bolts attached to me, they covered every inch of my body. Looping around my arms and torso, covering me in maroon light. The air filled with the strange stench of warm breakfast and frying meat. I thought I was going to die.

Hermia dropped the tumblers and the bottle of whisky and ran to kneel beside me.

"Don't fight," she said. "You can't stop it. Not now. So let it run its course and you might survive."

"Might?" I whined through gritted teeth. "What's happening?"

She didn't answer. But I knew it was bad news. My body convulsed as each new bolt connected to another part of me.

I couldn't ask her anything else. My mouth wrapped around hollow screams that filled my ears and throbbed through my skull.

The crackle of maroon threads encasing my face replaced my screaming and coated my vision filled with maroon bolts.

Hermia reached for my hand. Her expression soft, her brow pinched. "We're right here. We're not leaving you."

And then my awareness grayed from maroon to black and I fell unconscious to the sound of disjointed screams.

Kato's always said my screams haunted his dreams for months after the Inheritance. The smell of burning flesh had put him off barbecues for life.

Like Eden, I woke up in the Ancient Forest's Dryad City hospital after my Inheritance. Eden was sitting in a wooden rocking chair. Eleanor—her mother—told me later, Eden had kicked up a tremendous fuss, shouting and throwing electricity bolts until they'd let her into my room where she'd promptly curled up in the chair and fallen asleep.

She was the first thing I saw when I woke. Coiled up in the chair like a snail.

Eleanor came in and ushered a stream of Dryads who poked and prodded me, checking my vitals. When they'd finished and the last Dryad left, Eleanor turned to Eden.

"Honey, you have to leave now."

"Absolutely not. My best friend nearly died. I'm not going anywhere."

Eleanor sighed, her tiny frame sagged. She didn't want to fight with Eden.

"Can she come back after?" I asked.

"Of course."

Eden was already sassy at ten years old. She rolled her eyes. They had more violet in them by then, a few streaks, but some of the brown still remained.

"Fine. Look after him, can't be best friendless, can I?" She glanced at me and gave me a soft smile, which I tried to return though my face ached like hell. All of my body did. It was like I was lying on a bed of poisoned needles and fire embers. Every cell screamed and burnt.

Once Eden had shut the door, Eleanor pulled the rocking chair close to my bed and placed my hand between hers.

The problem with being a Siren, especially a Siren Fallon, is that you always know what's coming before it happens. No one can lie to you. No one can protect you from the truth. It stabs at your essence before they can suppress their emotions or distract themselves enough they don't project.

Eleanor tried, at least.

But Sirens spend so long reading and manipulating emotion we don't need to sense it to know what a person's feeling. Besides, having Inherited, I was far more powerful than a normal Fallon. It took me a long time to develop mechanisms to block out unwanted emotions. But it was the curve in Eleanor's expression that told me. Just like Eden, there was always so much written in their eyes.

"She's dead, isn't she?"

"That is the Council's assumption." She squeezed my arm as the first flood of tears rolled down my cheeks.

"Does Kato know?"

She shook her head. "We wanted to ask you whether you would like us to tell him or if you would prefer to talk to him."

"It should be me."

She rubbed her thumb over the back of my hand. It was meant to be comforting, but even that made my skin ache.

"What happened to me?"

"You Inherited her essence, we're not sure how."

"What does that mean?"

"It means you're extremely powerful and possibly Imbalanced."

FOUR

'Although the true origin of Dusting ceremonies has been lost to time, legend says they originated in the South state and were created because of a broken heart. A memory Siren mourned the loss of his Balancer for so long, he dug up her body and enlisted the help of a sorcerer to disintegrate her remains and essence into the powder we now call Dust. He then used his Siren abilities to cocoon himself inside a dome of her Dust and memories. He stayed there, reliving their life together until he too passed away from starvation.'

From the History of Forbidden and Lost Magic

More 2010 Memories, two or three months later, I forget exactly.

As the weeks drew on, it became embarrassing for the Council. Lani's physical body was still missing and my father still hadn't had a Dusting. So they promptly concluded two things:

First, I was to assume the duties of the Siren Fallon of the South immediately, and in order to do so, I had to be Bound, underage. No one was Bound before the age of sixteen. The Balance scriptures were too unreliable until then. That's why there was a Potential ceremony at sixteen and all Bindings occurred in the last year of Keepers school at eighteen. It was the only way "to be sure."

The second thing they concluded was that Lani must have died, therefore we needed a Dusting ceremony for both of them. Of course, without bodies, that was an impossibility. Our dear savior to the rescue. The First Fallon collected hair and trace particles of DNA from the mansion. She mixed it into some sort of "faux" Dust that had all the elements of Lani and Kale needed for the effects of the Dusting to appear authentic to the Siren population.

So that's how I came to stand in the middle of Siren city square, with a giant stage looming in front of me and a crowd that roared like the cries of a violent storm. I was wearing maroon suit trousers and a short-sleeved maroon top emblazoned with the Siren symbol. Kato was wearing a matching outfit. Neither of us wanted to wear suits. We were still children. I was a twelve-year-old boy-Fallon pretending to be adequate enough to be in charge, and Kato was only ten.

Kato stood by my side, holding my hand.

"Brother?" he said, squeezing. "You're doing it again."

"Huh?" I flinched. My torso was heaving, bubbles of heat frothed in my chest. After the Council determined Mom was, in fact, dead, the only thing it left me with was an intoxicating burn that consumed my body. It started between my ribs and filled my vision with red. It coursed through my ribs and into my veins, threading poison and shadows wherever it crept. Of course, it wasn't until after the Dusting we realized what I was feeling was Imbalance which had been created during the Inheritance. But no living person had seen an Inheritance, not the Council nor the Guild professors, none of us knew any better than the other. So it was all guesswork.

I didn't want to go on stage. I'd told Cecilia and begged Rafiq and Arden to make someone else do it because I wasn't ready. But they'd insisted. This was a Siren Fallon requirement, and I was now the Siren Fallon of the South. It wasn't a choice, this was duty. Rafiq was the family sorcerer, much like Arden was for Eden and her family. His long green robes flowed down his slender figure. Unlike Arden, he had no facial hair on his bronzed skin. And despite his age, he still stood straight and tall. The only thing time had touched were his eyes, that held a sadness that permeated all his expressions.

Kato walked me all the way to the stage, holding me tight the entire time. Cecilia and Rafiq greeted us and gestured for me to enter the stage through the curtains. They'd prepped me beforehand, so I knew what would happen and what I needed to do. Kato gripped my hand harder.

"Are you sure you're okay?" He lowered his voice. "It's peeling off you in killer waves. If I wasn't so impressed at the depths of your rage, I'd be mildly terrified. But I have a reaaally bad feeling about this."

I leaned in to give him a cuddle. "They haven't given me a choice."

He locked his arms around my waist. "Don't let it win. Keep control."

"I will."

And I really thought I would. Rafiq handed me a tiny maroon-colored pouch, which was so heavy I almost dropped it. I frowned at the bag, wondering why the hell it weighed so much when it was such a small pouch.

"Put the bag in the center of the stage. Eleanor's out there waiting for you. She'll summon wind to help the Dust out of the bag."

Rafiq held the stage curtains open, and bent to my ear as I passed. "Don't feel you have to say anything. You can just pull the Dust out and finish there. The Sirens will understand."

I nodded at him and glanced at Kato over my shoulder before I disappeared through the curtains.

I froze. The sun was low in the sky. Deep orange and pink daubed the horizon in long, thick streaks. It looked like burnt embers and sky flames. I've always loved the sunsets in the South. The only place they're more beautiful is the East. There is nothing like the desert for sunrise and sunset.

Thousands upon thousands of eyes focused on me as I stepped further onto the stage. Locked and latched on me like keys in a door. My breathing hitched up a notch. Somewhere behind the curtains, Kato reached out. His soft essence nudged at mine—a warning "chill out bro." I swallowed down the coarse lump in my throat, walked to the middle of the stage, and placed the bag on the ground.

Rafiq appeared on my left, to my right was Eleanor and behind her a band. The only thing in front of me was a CogMic and a few thousand Keepers. Cecilia floated through the crowd, the Keepers either side of her edging away to give her space. She settled near the front of the mass of Keepers. Her gaze was sharp. Sharper than the eyes of all the Keepers combined.

I reached for the CogMic. My hand shook around the cogs and metal mesh.

At my grandparents' Dusting two years prior, my father made a speech. It was short and powerful. The audience wept as his words wound through the air like smoke and glitter.

My throat was dry, no words were forming. I coughed. Shook my head and replaced the mic on the stand. I couldn't do what my father had done. There was no point trying. Instead, I glanced at the stage curtains, my parents' faces were embroidered on the velvet drapes. Huge, smiling and staring out at their adoring crowd.

Eleanor cleared her throat, and I acknowledged her. I was as ready as I could be. The pouch's drawstrings were silky. The bag slid open, a poof of maroon Dust wafted into the air. I stumbled back and collapsed on my butt. Several particles had caught on my nose and lips. I touched the places where they'd landed. My skin tingled.

Eleanor raised her hands, and the Dust shot into the atmosphere. The bag rippled and wobbled as a jet stream of maroon flew into the sky. The crowd erupted in a cacophony of cheers and hoots, excited squeals, and clapping.

The jet stream rose and rose and then burst like a fire-work. Dust particles arced, fanning out into a dome shape.

As the dome descended, so too did a maroon mist over my vision. I had no idea what was happening. The curtains ruffled behind me. Kato appeared.

"Trey? What the hell?"

But it was too late. Kato's voice muted to a whisper. The maroon haze consumed my body. It flooded my veins in hot, spitting bubbles. My eyes slammed shut. I tried to focus on shutting down the rage pumping through my veins like adrenaline. But the harder I fought, the more it controlled me.

It wasn't fair. We'd lost everything, and I was having to stand here doing ridiculous duties when I should have been cradling my brother and telling him it was okay. I didn't want any of this. I just wanted to curl into a ball and sleep until the pain subsided.

I was standing. But I couldn't remember getting up. My arms raised out in front of me as if I was conducting an opera. Strange.

I looked up. The dome was half made, still high in the sky but crawling ever closer to the ground. When it sealed, it would lock everyone in the city-dome for three days. No one in or out.

No. I didn't want to stay there.

Blood filled my ears. It thumped and rushed against the roar of my breath. I had to leave and go to the Ancient Forest, surrounded by trees and water and stillness. I needed to be with Eden.

The crowd's cheers crescendoed. The band beat out rhythmic thuds. I wanted it to stop. I needed everything to just. Stop.

Everywhere I looked was maroon. Every inch of my body was hot. My skin was on fire. I wanted to throw things and break things. I wanted to end things.

Something silent snapped. I remember thinking it was odd how the quiet things can be so devastating. The snap ripped through my insides, tore my mind in two, severed any rational thought. My vision narrowed, I swear I grew physically, my muscles expanded, I rose off the stage, my body hummed with power.

Someone called my name. But it was muffled, irrelevant. All I wanted was to break things. The maroon staining my vision deepened. My hands twitched. And then there was blissful silence.

Time stretched. The silent beat was thick, comforting. It wrapped me in peace and the solitude I'd been craving. But the crowd's collective eyes jerked to me. The cheering halted. Even my breathing stilled.

Then one long, ringing shriek ripped through the city and shattered the silence. Scream after scream filled the air. Hands reached for faces and ears. Keepers dropped to the floor.

They were breaking. Good. I wanted to break things. I needed to end things like my parents. They were dead, and it wasn't fair. Someone had to pay. I didn't care who. I didn't care about anything. My body was too far away. Everything was. Even the crowd. They weren't people anymore. They were cogs and machinery. What did it matter if I broke them? My outstretched hands clenched into fists. The screaming ricocheted around the square. Pieces of machinery dropped to the floor in front of me. I zeroed in on one tiny cog. There, that one I could break slowly, bending and twisting until it cracked in two. Then it was still and relief washed throughout my body.

The air was chilly, filled with ice and goosebumps. Slithers of dark shadows and nightmares coming true slipped through the crowd in maroon and black wisps. I smiled as cogs twitched and dropped to the floor and writhed. Arms and legs all twisted at wrong angles like dead spiders.

There was a hand on my arm. I shook it off. It gripped my elbow. Tugged. A cool wave pushed its way inside my chest. Siren magic. Compulsion.

A little voice pierced through it all.

"It hurts. Make it stop."

Kato.

Just as suddenly as the maroon mist had descended over my vision, it evaporated.

I bent double. Gasping for oxygen. I grabbed at Kato's arm. His eyes were enormous and round. Tears and blood streaked his face. His nose was dripping.

"I had to stop you," he said, shaking his head and wiping his face.

"What the hell did you do?"

I looked back at the crowd. The first ten rows of people were on the floor, motionless. Unconscious, I hoped. The rest had backed away. Many of them running screaming to get out of the dome's reach before it sealed us all in.

"We have to leave," I said.

"One of us has to stay. You go," Kato said.

In the middle of the bodies beneath the stage was a small boy. He was lying on his back. His eyes were as wide as Kato's, but his skin was pale. His chest still.

No.

I leapt off the stage and ran to where he rested. He was so small, his limbs tiny. He couldn't be more than five or six years old. I clamped his nose shut and pushed two breaths into his lungs. Then I balled my fists and pumped his ribs up and down.

"Breathe damn it."

But he didn't. He didn't do a goddamn thing. He was forever resting in a world of terrors and demons.

Kato gripped my shoulders.

"You need to leave."

I wiped a hand over my face. My skin was slick with tears. What had I done?

I scanned the crowd one more time and caught Cecilia's narrowed eyes. She focused directly on me.

"TREY," Kato bellowed. His fists slammed into my chest, knocking me onto my back.

"Go."

So I did. I got up and ran. And left everyone behind. The Dust-dome was two feet from the floor as I slid under it and it crashed into the pavement, sealing the chaos in for three days.

I lay on the cold cobbled floor, taking deep shuddering breaths until I heard footsteps. Then I ran and ran. I stole a hooded jacket from a storefront and boarded a public train, and then when it reached the Ancient Forest, I continued running until I arrived at The Pink Lake. It was only when I was there, alone and safe, that I let the tears out.

Giant sobs that cracked open my chest and devoured pieces of my soul. I was horrified, mortified as shame burrowed into my skin.

When my tears had run dry, I pulled out my CogTracker and texted Kato.

How many?

Do you really want to know the answer to that?

How many, Kato?

Twelve.

The boy?

They couldn't save him.

I didn't text back for a while. I couldn't. How was I supposed to live with this? I placed my fingertips on my temples and pulled. A silk thread came loose and spun in my palm, forming a ball. I pulled until the entire memory danced before me. I replayed the event over and over. Until the ache in my chest subsided and I could watch without tears.

Something was wrong with me. I was broken, a vault had cracked in my mind, it had let loose demons and darkness, monsters and evils. None of which I could control.

The only word I had to describe it was: Imbalance.

FIVE

'Memory Balls: A memory ball containing the memories from another Keeper. Made of Dust. Usually stable, and if the Siren is skillful enough, then transferable between Keepers. Though legal, they are viewed as morally dubious and often frowned upon, as memories impact and shape a Keepers personality.'

The Dictionary of Balance

Memories from Late 2014

I Inherited when I was twelve. But other than the Dusting outburst, I didn't exhibit any more signs of Imbalance until I was older. It could have been the hormones, or maybe I'd just had enough. But once the fragments of Imbalance appeared, The First Fallon jumped on me. She announced my "apprenticeship" as if it was some divine opportunity. It was total bullshit, of course. An excuse to do what she called "experiments" on me.

What she actually did was torture my sixteen-year-old self until the vault I'd carefully constructed in the depths of my mind to hold all the Imbalance split open. It was all some warped test to see how much damage I created. She's sick, a sociopathic god, hellbent on torturing kids.

I realize now she was afraid of what I could do to her. But that's not important. What's important is how I ended the torture. And why it might be the only advantage we have against her.

Hermia was drinking. She was in the bar that I eventually took over. I shouldn't have been in there, given my age, but as the Siren Fallon, no one was kicking me out either. Though the then owner, Silas, also didn't let me drink anything I shouldn't.

I was holding a glass of pop. Hermia was cradling a whiskey.

"She doesn't know I can do it," I said.

"Do what, exactly?" Hermia said. Her orange eyes blade thin.

"Ask her. Ask Cecilia about yesterday. She doesn't remember what happened."

"Is that so?" Hermia drew every syllable out.

"Don't pull that tone with me. I don't know how I did it. But I know I wiped her memory. That's how I—"

"How you saw Eden?"

I glance up at her, a question in the curve of my brow. She tutted at me.

"Lest you forget, I am the greatest tracker this world has ever known. I always know where your scrawny ass is."

"She forbade me from seeing her."

"I know."

My fingers gripped the glass I was holding. Hermia's eyes slid down to my whitened knuckles and then up to meet my stare. She sipped her whiskey, never breaking eye contact.

"It was an accident. I was so cross with Cecilia for forbidding me from seeing Eden that I just cracked. It was like I had all this extra power but not from the vault; this was different. It wasn't dark, it was protective."

"It might be your way out of this mess, you know."

"What do you mean?"

She shrugged. "No one knows what you're capable of, right? Not even her. So keep wiping her memory. Then, when you're good enough, wipe everything. All the torture, all the apprenticeship, the whole thing."

"I don't know. It cost me so much energy, I passed out. She's too powerful. It took everything I had just to wipe those few minutes."

She leaned forward, resting her chin on her folded arms, her whiskey glass nestled in the crook of her elbow. "Do it again. Intentionally this time, though."

"I don't know what happened the first time, let alone how to manage it again."

"Well, that's your problem. Figure it out, but... and this is important. Only once a week. And only when I'm around. If I'm there, I can help weave the lies. This is a gift. You need to be careful with it. And for the love of fuck, don't let her find out what you're doing."

So that's what I did. Each week I'd practice trying to steal another memory from her. Hermia would sneak me out and get Magnus to take me home. She would also slip messages to Eden via some Elementals.

It took me about two months to gain control of it. And another six to master it. Long enough for Cecilia to cover my back in scars from all the whippings and cuttings. Eve always had an issue with my scars. But it's funny, it wasn't them that bothered me; it was what Cecilia did to my insides that hurt. She'd implant visions to fuck with my memories, so I didn't know what was real or imagined or my own warped Imbalance. Over and over she'd implant memories of me killing Eden, or hurting her in violent, awful ways. And always by my own hand.

I'd met Hermia in the bar. It was something of a habit. She would drink, I would pry her for information, though she rarely gave me much about herself. Only the occasional nugget about her son and husband. So instead, we'd focus on my training and the control I was building. Hermia was always so invested. I guess now I'm in Obex, I realize why. She had a vested interest in taking Cecilia down, given she'd put Bellamy here.

One day, Cecilia had provided me with an array of particularly disgusting images of me killing Eden's parents, slicing their stomachs open in front of Eden and letting their innards spill to the floor as the tears that streaked Eden's face turned to blood trails. But that wasn't what hurt. What had hurt was the expression Eden had pulled. A mangled twist of disgust and hatred. I never wanted Eden to look at me like that. It tipped me over the edge and I'd demanded Hermia meet me earlier than planned.

"I don't appreciate changing the plan," Hermia barked as she slipped into the booth seat.

"I know. But I'm done. She doesn't get to do this to me anymore."

Hermia's shoulders went rigid. "Listen, boy, you have neither the control nor the power to end things yet. You could kill yourself trying."

I looked up at her, my glare hard. "If that's what it takes, then so be it."

Hermia slammed her fist down on the table so suddenly I jumped back in my seat.

"NO," she barked. And then shook herself, patting her hair down. "You don't get to die... Not yet."

I reached out and wrapped my hand around her fist. It broke the haze she was in and she met my gaze.

"I can't do this anymore. I need it to stop."

She slouched in her chair; her face softer, the fire that had blared through her gaze dampened to embers.

"I know. Do you think I don't know that? Do you think I enjoy watching her torture you? I should be able to do something. To stop her, fight her. Something. Anything."

"So help me end it. I've been thinking, I don't need to take all her memories from the last few months. That's too obvious. It would leave an enormous hole in her memory and she'd know something was missing. We have to be more subtle than that."

"I'm listening."

"Rather than me using the memory wipe like a sledge-hammer, I need to be surgical. Excise out just the torture memories and the memories relating to her decision to create this fake apprenticeship. If I remove them all, the idea vanishes and she won't realize the memories of those events are missing."

Hermia's eyes curled at the corners, her mouth pinched into a vicious smile.

"That, I like. A lot. It just might work. How much do you think you need to take?"

"Still more than I've ever taken before, but I think I can do it."

"When?"

"A week from now."

"Okay," she said.

That was how it was supposed to go. I don't know whether Cecilia sniffed something amiss, whether it was an awful coincidence or perhaps the Balance really is a duplicitous bastard. But we never made it to the end of the week.

Hermia was in the corner of Cecilia's office, scowling and smeared in something dark. I didn't ask what, too exhausted from Cecilia's torture.

I slumped in an office chair, my back and arms covered in welts. She'd been extra brutal that day because I didn't break. She hated it when she couldn't break me and it had been happening more and more. In a strange way, the more she hurt me, the more it taught me to control my power and the stronger the vault got.

Cecilia sat back in her chair, her dress split, showing the white of her thigh. She was white like milk and vampires, snow and acid. Other than her dress, the only thing she wore was a sneer.

"You're going to be Bound," she said. Her words smooth like honey and silk, she bordered on compulsion. That shit doesn't work on me, though. So she could compel all she wanted. I wasn't playing.

"Yes. To Eden," I said. That was a mistake. I shouldn't have opened my mouth.

The sneer stretched wide open, like the cracking of an egg. She was all edges and claws.

"No dear. You were never going to be Bound to Eden. That was one of those unfortunate friendships. A delusion, if you like."

She laughed. It was dry, full of steel and venom.

Bitter prickles attacked my essence. Her poisonous

emotions sour and acrid. They ran down my spine, my breath caught.

"No," I shouted. "No." I was standing. Panting, my eyes darkened, the vault broken wide open. I couldn't, or didn't, want to stop it. I let the vault walls crumble until power coursed through my veins and throbbed in my grip.

Cecilia stood too. Her face curled into a thin smile. She wanted this. Wanted the reaction. She failed to elicit it in her torture chamber, so she tried a different tactic in her office.

"You don't get to control me anymore," I snarled. "We're done."

"We're done when I say we're done." She rose in the air, floating a few feet off the ground.

I snorted, "You don't scare me. I've seen inside you, Cecilia. You're empty. Alone with your broken ideals. You'll never be happy. You don't know what happiness is."

She faltered, one small wrinkle on her perfectly smooth brow.

I reached out, threw both hands forward. Hermia scrambled out of her chair.

"You said a week," she shouted. It was too late. Cecilia had pushed too far. She wasn't Binding me to someone else. She wouldn't have the satisfaction of torturing me for an infinite number of lifetimes.

I dug deep, pulling on my essence, focusing it all on Cecilia. Her memories tasted like a plague. They were cruel and intense, coated in watery sorrow. I yanked and tore images and visions out of her. Something wet ran down my nose. I wiped it on my shoulder, a blood-red smear streaking my top. It didn't matter. I couldn't stop. Not now. I had to carry on. I had to take it all, or she'd realize what I'd done and it would be for nothing.

I was on my knees. The effort was draining me of everything I had. I took more and more. Weaving her memories into a giant ball that evaporated into the air as fast as I created it. A constant flickering of dust and white smoke. My vision blurred.

Cecilia was trembling on her feet. Blood dripped in slow, rhythmic beads from her eyes and ears. It stained her cream dress, her cream floor. A hazy expression glossed over her features.

"Trey," Hermia shrieked. That's the only time I've ever heard her shriek. I wiped my face. Trickles of blood fell from my nose. It was killing me.

"STOP," Hermia bellowed. But I couldn't, I was so close. I reached into Cecilia one last time, tearing the final most precious fragment. The idea, her desire to examine the Imbalance inside me. My vision darkened. My hold on the memory slipped.

I fell into the dark comfort of nothingness.

I didn't know until the following day when I'd woken in Hermia's apartment that I'd gotten it. Hermia had to drag Cecilia to her bed and leave her there, while she rushed me to her apartment. I'd been unconscious for hours. She'd wiped my face clean and kept me comfortable. When I woke, Hermia told me about Cecilia. Apparently, she was in a state of dazed confusion, but thankfully had no memory of torturing me. And then she dropped the bombshell.

"But, Trey..." Her voice faded. She swallowed and held my hand before she spoke. "You took the torture and the idea, but you didn't take the idea of her Binding you. She's even more set on Binding you to someone other than Eden. She's found a girl from a different realm. I'm so sorry."

My heart dropped, my stomach sank. "Then it was all for nothing."

"Don't say that. She was torturing you. Saving you from that is everything."

"Not if I can't be with Eden."

I went straight to the Pink Lake to meet Eden. Magnus dropped me as close as he could, and I ran the rest of the way. But when I found Eden, she was sitting with her knees bunched under her chin, tears soaking her cheeks.

All the excitement of seeing her fizzled out instantly.

"Eden?" I breathed. "What the hell is wrong?"

She wiped her sleeve over her face. I crouched next to her and sat on the lake's edge in amongst the soft pink leaves. It was the first time I slid my arm around her. I wanted to stop her tears even though I knew the knowledge I was harboring would likely create more. I'd cried enough over it.

I pulled her in tight. She was warm, but there was a pointed, sour wave peeling off her.

"What's happened?" I said.

"Victor."

"What's the little prick done this time?"

She sniffed out a muffled laugh. Her eyes glistened with tears, but at least she was smiling.

"Not him. I overheard my parents."

My chest tightened. A sharp stab dug into my ribs. I already knew I didn't want to hear what she was going to say any more than she would want to hear about my impending Binding.

"They're saying I'm going to be Bound to Victor. The Council, everyone has said he's the most likely candidate to be called as my Potential." Her voice cracked on the last word. I bit my lip hard enough to suppress the scream tearing up my insides.

She turned to me, tears welled, "Victor? Seriously?"

I couldn't look at her because I already knew I was going to be Bound to someone else. I just didn't know it was Eve until later.

I slipped my hand into hers.

"I always thought I'd be Bound to you," she said.

"Me too. We've spent our entire lives thinking that. Don't you think it's a little odd that we're made for each other and yet every other couple like us are rumored to be Potentials, but we're not?"

She snuggled into my shoulder, her head fit perfectly under my chin, as if that's where she was always meant to be.

"Are we deluded?"

"What does your soul tell you?"

She stayed silent.

"Exactly. Mine too. Something is wrong. There has to be a reason all this is happening for no reason."

"All? What do you mean?"

I stiffened, let go of her hand, and inched away. I had to tell her that night. Our meetings were so sporadic I didn't know when I'd see her again and the chances were that it would be after I was Bound already.

"I..."

"Trey? What is it? You're scaring me."

My head hung low. I ran my hand over my face, trying to find the words to explain.

"The First Fallon... she's found someone to Bind me to."

The silence that sat between us was as vast as all the oceans. Eden took several deep breaths. Waves of emotion peeled off her. First searing heat bubbles. They pumped hard and fast, rising in a crescendo of ash and smoke and fire. I wondered if I'd have to compel her into calmness. But as soon as I had the thought, all the heat and froth vanished.

Instead, she hollowed out, an empty void punctuated by a cold so penetrating, I shivered. She was blocking me out.

"That's it then?" she said.

I didn't answer because what could I say? Anything I said would have hurt more, torn more pieces of us.

"I don't want it."

"You don't need to say that. It's fine. You're obviously fated to be with her and I to Victor."

"Am I though? I don't believe that. None of this makes sense."

"He disgusts me. He's putrid. You know he killed my fucking dog. How am I supposed to be Bound to someone like that?"

"Didn't you break his arms for that?"

"Not the point."

"I don't even know the girl I'm supposedly meant to be Bound to. Hermia says she's come from another realm. You ever heard of someone being Bound to a Keeper from another realm? I haven't."

She dropped her head, then turned to face me.

"I guess this is it, then?" she said.

"It will never be it, Eden. Don't you get it? I don't care who I'm Bound to, my heart will always be yours."

"You can't know that. Bindings change everything. You'll fall in love with her. I'll be a distant memory, a family friend. A wistful childhood memory of times that once were."

I pressed my lips shut. The thought of that terrified me.

"I don't want to love him," she said, her voice cracking. "He's vile."

I leaned my forehead against hers, drinking in the smell of desert and summer and fresh lightning.

She shifted back. Our lips were so close, I wanted to kiss

her, my whole body willed itself forward. But I was frozen. Her hand came to my cheek. She held me in her palm.

"I thought this was real."

"It is real. You know it's real."

"How, Trey? How do I know it's real when The First Fallon, The Council and Fate itself is telling us otherwise?"

"It's real because of how much it hurts."

"We have to stop this," she said. "We can't live a life in shadows and secrets. What kind of life is that?"

"W—"

"No. Stop. We're fated to live these lives. Apart. I can't be in your life if you're Bound to someone else. It will hurt too much."

"It's worth it if we get more time together."

She shook her head, tears streaking her face. "I have to go."

She kissed me on the forehead and walked away, leaving me alone by the Pink Lake.

SIX

'There are nine known realms: Trutinor, Obex, Earth, Dragoory, Eldervoor, Devanire, Clarvin, Janorth, and Lusveer.'

The Historical Geography of the Nine Realms, Vol. 4

Memories from Late 2014

The first time I met Eve, I was sixteen. Cecilia ensured Kato was with a nanny so that she and Eve had my full attention. Cecilia was weary of me for a while after I'd taken such a significant amount of her memories. It was like a part of her knew something was off, and she knew it was my fault, but she couldn't quite place the what or how. Good. I wanted the evil bitch rattled. I wanted doubt sowing seeds in her unconscious mind. She might have godlike power, but every god has a weakness. She needed to know that. But this memory isn't about Cecilia or how I'm going to exact revenge. This is about Evelyn.

Hermia waltzed unannounced into Cecilia's office with a tall girl dressed in green robes. Hermia's face was, as usual, a picture of suppressed rage. At least she was on my team—the scowl she wore was so fierce, I knew she didn't want to deliver a girl to me any more than I wanted to receive her. As I caught Hermia's eye, her skin quivered like earthquakes and thunder.

Eve bundled into the room in front of Cecilia like a golden trophy. Dressed in rich green silks embroidered with the symbol of the West. I raised an eyebrow. She wasn't from the West; she was from another realm, although I'd been told she was a distant relative of Arden's.

"I guess we'll leave you two to get to know each other for a while," Cecilia sneered with every word she said. Her white skin taut against her face. Though it was me who was smug that day. I took a great pleasure in watching the shiver when she looked at me. I'd put that tremble behind her eyes. She wasn't okay. I'd unnerved her, and she didn't know why.

"Your Binding is in a week's time," Cecilia spat and marched out of the room, nodding for Hermia to follow. Hermia gave me one hard stare and then left with a grunt.

Eve took a seat on Cecilia's big office sofa. It was white, a Chesterfield that was uncomfortable as hell. All Chester-fields are, though that doesn't stop me furnishing my house in them. I love the way they curl at the corners and the uniform buttons.

My stomach was in knots as I sat opposite Eve. I wasn't sure what was stronger, the urge to vomit or the twitch in my muscles begging me to flee. I took a deep breath and looked at the girl. She was beautiful, in a cold way. Her eyes were a watery green, her hair the color of midday sunlight. Her face was oval and bright. She was pretty and her smiling expression seemed kind. Could I spend my life with her?

Another thought smashed through—she wasn't Eden. When every cell in your body screams that your soul mate is someone else, who do you listen to? Fate or your own instincts? How was I—a sixteen-year-old child—supposed to break a millennia old tradition? Trutinor had built its very foundations on fate and trust in Cecilia.

"Where's your family?" I asked.

"Gone," she said, her features pale and cool.

Dead? Like mine. Or just in another realm? I scanned her face, reached out, stretching until the prickle of her feelings latched onto my essence. I wanted to understand how she felt about family. Honestly, I think that was the only time I ever saw her vulnerable. A wave of tense bristles peeled off her. They tasted tart, edged with licorice. But as fast as I'd connected with her emotions, they changed. Everything shut down. Her eyes hardened, shifting from watery green to ice cold.

"She took me from them," she whispered. "Said I wasn't to think of them anymore, that you were my family."

She paused. Something so dark washed through her expression it made me shift in my seat. I guess Cecilia wasn't the only one who was unnerved.

"Are you?" she asked, her voice sweet like clouds and candy.

"Am I what?"

Her emotions flipped again. I frowned; I couldn't keep up. Her feelings kept switching on and off. Warmth flooded her cheeks, her eyes swelled big and round.

"My family, silly?"

I wavered, my essence still reeling from her whiplash emotions. How was I supposed to know? I was young.

Despite Kato and I recovering from the initial shock of losing our parents a few years prior, their deaths had left a gaping hole in our lives. A void so deep nothing I did filled it.

I was trying to "father" and "brother" Kato and not doing a great job of either. Too much of a brother to be a father and trying too hard to be a father to be a good brother. Back then, I made a point of not knowing much. All I could do was fight through each day. The next Council meeting, the next Siren matter. Kato's latest school report, my private tutoring exams. Kato was the only actual family I had left. Eden too. Eden who I'd never be Bound to because of this girl sitting before me.

What was Eve expecting from me? To swear my life to hers? All my lives? We were talking about our souls for Balancesake and I'd only just met her. I realize now everything she said was wrong. Even then—especially then—the whole situation was one big Cecilia-shaped manipulation. I was blind, wrapped in the system, exactly where Cecilia wanted me. Now I know how deep her manipulation goes. I should have listened to my gut and the itch that was threading its way through my veins. Perhaps if I had. Perhaps if I'd said something, anything other than what I did, I wouldn't have hurt Eden and Cecilia would be dead instead of me.

But all I said was, "I—"

Eve reached out and held my hand. Pulsing beneath her skin was the same whiplash of emotions I'd already felt. The faint hint of something sour, and an overwhelming cool summer breeze washed over me. Flecked with sweet pops and dandelions, it was the tingled anticipation of hope that got to me. Eve was hurting, but there was still an innocent girl under the resentment and the soft innocence was intoxicating. I'd lost so much, said goodbye to too many loved ones. I didn't want to lose anything else. Whether I wanted to be Bound to Eve or not. She was mine and represented a chance to do things right. She made me want to protect her. So that's what I did.

"I'll always look after you," I said.

It's the only real promise I've ever made to her. It's the only one I didn't keep.

We were Bound a week later, just like Cecilia said. It was uneventful. Only key Council members in attendance. No big audience, unlike most Binding ceremonies. Just me, Eve, Cecilia and a handful of stuffy old Keepers.

It hurt like hell, the Binding. It wasn't like mine and Eden's—that felt like the sun kissing the ocean, like static and summer heat, winter blankets and golden hearth fires.

Once it was over, Eve's face exploded into a golden grin. It blazed across her face. She looked like sunshine and raindrops. Like snow and luscious green meadows all at the same time.

I'm not sure whether it was the Binding or the way she stared at me like I was all the atoms inside the universe, but I knew then I loved her. I loved her like family, like comfort, and like home.

I also knew I wasn't in love with her and I never would be because she wasn't Eden. Even though I was Bound to Eve, I was still *in* love with Eden. That should have been enough to tell me something was wrong with our Binding. But when you've grown up in a world where fate can't be questioned, it's a hard thing to rebel against. Just one more failure in a long list of them.

A month later, Eve and I were on my bed. Her gold hair flowed around her shoulders; her fingers laced through mine. I hated the way she touched me. Always gentle, her caress tender. The slip of her skin against mine meant everything to her and nothing to me. I couldn't reconcile the two, so I spent our days clamping my essence down. I didn't want to sense her burgeoning emotions pushing against me. It was suffocating. Everything we were living was a lie, and one she refused to acknowledge.

Did I leave my CogTracker out for her to find? Maybe she was just sly about reading my messages. Maybe it was a little of both.

"Who are you sending so many CogMessages to?" she asked. Her tone was light, full of innocence and joy.

My stomach tightened. I sat up, unlocking my fingers from hers.

"Oh, no one. Just boring Council stuff." The lie slipped off my tongue like oil.

I'm a good liar. Most Sirens are. It's too easy for us to camouflage our feelings. To press truths into shadows and whispers. Eve should have been a Siren. She was a far better liar than me. The warmth I was accustomed to drained from her face. Her eyebrows sharpened, her stare intensified like bullets and glass.

"Really?" she drawled. "Then who is Eden?"

My hands went cold. I glanced at my CogTracker. It was sitting between us, and I hadn't put it there. That was the thing about Eve. I'd learned quickly that everything she did was calculated, a manipulation. Always gaming and playing you to get what she wanted, whether that was love, information or a soul mate. I reached out, but her hand was already there.

"Don't lie to me, Trey. I've already read the messages. I know you have feelings for her." This was a tone I'd never heard. It was venomous and acidic.

"She's an old friend." Truth. And a lie.

Eden was an old friend, but she was so much more.

"You're mine. Not hers," Eve said, her blade-like words pricked at the air.

"I know."

"Do you though?" She held out my CogTracker, dangled it in front of me like it was a sweet.

"I miss you." She waggled the tracker, her voice faux deep. "I want to meet you, but things are difficult."

"Don't mock me, Eve. You have no fucking idea who—"

"Don't mock you? Are you fucking kidding me? I left my family, my realm, my entire world to be here for you and you tell me not to mock you?"

I sighed and reached for the tracker. She yanked her arm back and launched it into the air. I ducked. I still don't know if she was throwing it at me or the wall.

It smashed. The explosion ripped through the room as it broke into a thousand pieces. Each cog a tiny lie, or a midnight message, or a whispered phone call. All of them to Eden.

"Was that really necessary? They're expensive to replace."

"And you're wealthy. What does it matter?"

"What do you want from me, Eve?"

"I want everything. Don't you get it? I want you. All of you. Not the bit you can afford to give me. Not scraps of your emotions and love. I WANT ALL OF YOU."

I closed my mouth. I didn't want to fight, we'd been Bound a month, our days should be full of laughter and finding out about each other.

"What do you want from me? What can I do to make it better?"

"I don't want you talking to her."

I sucked in a breath. That was the one thing I couldn't give her. So I said nothing.

She screamed, flinging her hands up. "Don't you get it? You're my everything. This is it for me. I don't get to go home."

I opened my mouth to respond, but she cut me off.

"No, I'm talking. I'd do anything to make you smile and prosper and keep you happy. I'm standing by your side, the perfect doting queen, and it's still not enough. What else do I need to do? I'm doing everything I can..." she trailed off. Eventually, she looked up at me. Tears filled her eyes. "It's never going to be enough for you, is it? Do you know how that makes me feel? Jesus, Trey. You haven't even kissed me for Balancesake."

I hadn't. I didn't really want to either. The only person I wanted to kiss was hundreds of miles away in the West. Her body sagged. All the heat from her rage seeped out, hitting me in ever softer ebbs. She inched closer, picked up my hands, and locked her slender fingers between mine.

"Can you try to be with me?" she pleaded.

She inched closer. Her lips brushed against mine. They were smooth and warm. My crotch responded, even if my heart didn't. Her gaze dropped to my pants, then slowly crawled their way up my body.

"Oh, so you do have some feelings for me, at least."

I gave her a limp smile. My insides were squirming. Her beauty was fierce. I was Bound to her. It was inevitable we'd have to be together, eventually sleep together. Other than my groin, nothing moved. I couldn't touch her, hold her, or bring myself to kiss her.

So, like everything with Eve, she pushed and shoved and led me where she wanted me. And I let her.

Her hand traced my jaw line and around the back of my

neck. She pulled me close. Her other hand guided mine to her leg. She pushed up. My hand slid over her smooth skin until it met the pinch of lace and cotton between her legs.

"Have you ever?" she breathed.

I shook my head. When would I have had the chance? My life was Kato and Council meetings and torture. And when it wasn't those things, it was Eden.

"Go slow, okay?" she said.

I swallowed hard and nodded. She pressed my fingers inside her and slipped her lips over mine. And I tried my hardest not to think of Eden.

SEVEN

'The rarest Siren ability is that of the Memory Keeper. And perhaps that is the Balance's way of protecting Keepers. After all, we are but the product of our memories. If they are changed, manipulated or altered, then who do we become?'

Professor Aldridge, *The History of Sirenism*

November 30, 2016

I don't like regrets. They're insidious little worms. They eat away, grinding you down until you acknowledge the trouble you're in. Until ~~you~~—I—acknowledge that everything I thought was right and just and moral was a lie. But I'm dead now, so I figure when better to reflect on life and let go of the regrets than right now?

For a while, this memory was special because I had both sides of it. I kept it buried in the recesses of my essence; I'd only pull out the memories when I was alone. Back then, I'd spin up specks of black and purple Dust and laced between her memories were particles of maroon Dust—my version of the same memory. I've always loved how the Dust memories spin and pulse like they're alive.

Now, though, the Dust memory is vivid maroon, with only the tiniest flecks of black and lilac remaining. Those flecks of black and lilac are the only parts of Eden I have. The only part of her I'll have for a century. I guess I should tell you what happened and why my most precious memory is home to the only regret I've ever had...

Eden's birthday was the day before her Potential ceremony. I'd woken up with a tension headache, probably because I'd spent the previous week flip-flopping over what to do. Eve knew something was off. She'd mostly kept her distance and buried herself in schoolwork. I rolled over. Eve was gone already. I sagged in bed, relieved I didn't have to pretend anything this morning. Now I look back, I realize how much of an asshole I was. I didn't care what Eve felt. Not when it came to Eden. Eve and I had come to a silent agreement. She knew there was no way I could ever give all of myself to her, but I gave her the pieces of me that I could.

Don't get me wrong, I loved her. When she died, there was a small piece of me that ached for the loss, the companionship. But that morning, all that mattered was she'd gone somewhere, and I was alone. I picked up my CogTracker and dropped Eden a message.

Good morning birthday girl, how did you sleep? I hope you're being spoiled this morning.

Hey, you. I am indeed. Though Nyx is still running around flapping, trying to get me to choose a dress for the ceremony tomorrow. But I give zero fucks. I can't stand the thought of choosing something when getting on stage is the last thing I want to do.

How are you anyway?

Been better. I want to see you today.

Do you think that's wise given tomorrow?

It's your birthday. There's no way I'm not seeing you.

Fine. But not with her. I don't have the strength to play happy Fallons today.

Tonight then?

Fine by me. Usual place?

11pm. Can't have cinders out too late the night before her special day.

Fuck off.

Ha. See you tonight.

I put my CogTracker down and climbed into the

shower. Between Council meetings and dealing with Kato, the day passed in a whirl. Kato spent much of the morning pacing the mansion and sending out waves of intensely irritating anxiety prickles. Every time he walked past my office, I'd get stabbed with pin-like anxiety.

"Shouldn't you be at school?" I barked.

"Couldn't stand it," he called back. "Train is ready to leave in an hour."

Most families would stay at Keepers school. Council members and Fallons usually stayed at the Council because there was always some business to deal with before a big ceremony.

Kato stuck his head through my office door. He was biting his lip, his brow furrowed in a dozen lines.

"Would you chill out? You quite literally have nothing to worry about."

"You don't know that."

I couldn't summon the energy to argue with him.

"I'm dropping you back at school before I head to the Ancient Forest this evening."

"But—"

"No buts. Back to school, I have stuff to deal with tonight."

He stuck his middle finger up at me and sauntered out. Cocky little bastard.

Eve arrived home later in the day but stayed in the South because she had too much work to do.

So I left her, quietly pleased that I didn't have to escape her later on. I don't remember now what the evening Council meeting was about. Nothing interesting—were they ever?

I crept through the Forest, alight with the lack of emotion in the atmosphere. It was what I loved most about

The Pink Lake. There were so few Keepers around that the air only vibrated from the chirp of insects. Dew and breeze touched my skin instead of a cacophony of emotions. Being around Keepers is exhausting. They rarely moderate themselves. Allowing their feelings to spill out, roll through the atmosphere like they've no secrets to hide. Kato loves people. He's far better at dealing with the onslaught of their emotions. I've always thought he'd be better as a Siren Fallon of the South than me.

She's not there when I arrive. So I take a few moments just to sit and be still. The lake is beautiful. A fine layer of pink petals, blossom and tree shedding covered the top of the lake. It was a protective blanket for the fish and creatures that lurked below. The only interruption to the sea of pink was the occasional lily pad. A few minutes later, there was a rustle in the trees, and a head full of curls and bright lilac eyes appeared. She smiled, big, wide—so happy to see me, and yet something inside me crumbled. I stood up, and we ran to each other.

She flung her arms around me. It had been a while since we'd physically seen each other alone. There were occasions, big, formal State occasions when we were both in the same room. There might have been a stolen conversation, the odd glance. But we hadn't been alone together in forever. I drank in every inch of her as I bundled her up in my arms, pressing myself against her. Inhaling the scent of desert and sun from her skin. I swam in the intoxication of her. She was summer warmth, always a little hotter than comfortable and a strange mix of sweet, laced with static and a hint of fire smoke. Her emotions were my favorite smell.

I touched her cheek, savoring every second of her eyes locked on mine.

"Eden..." I started, but I didn't know how to finish my sentence. There were so many things I wanted to say to her —so many things I couldn't.

"Wait..." she said and pressed her hand against mine.

The pressure of wanting something I couldn't have built inside me. Half of me knew it was futile. But words poured out of my mouth before I could stop them.

"No. I don't want to wait anymore; I love you. Only you. Always you."

I leaned in, her breath trickled over mine. Her sweet fire-smoke and static filled my lungs. God, I wanted her so bad. I craved every inch of her, from her untameable hair to her determination and even the bickering. She was meant to be my Balancer, I knew it then as much as I know it now. She drew every ounce of me toward her, as if she already were a part of me.

I pulled her close. My mouth hovered over hers. This was a betrayal to Eve. But my heart and soul wanted Eden. I wavered, wondering what would happen if Eve found out. Did I even care? If I had to spend my life with Eve, I wanted to do it knowing what a kiss from Eden was like. If she kissed me and I felt nothing, I guessed I'd have my answer. But if she kissed me and it was everything, I'd know The First Fallon had meddled. Eden was worth any consequence that came out of this.

Our lips brushed, and then I kissed her.

Her skin against mine was oxygen to my soul, my nerves were electric, my essence trembled with the heat from her body so close to mine. My heart was thunder and lightning and a thousand crashing waves. She was life, this moment, this kiss was everything. It was the perfect memory, in the perfect place. And then I ruined it.

She pulled away. Her lips close enough. The millimeters of air between us crackled.

Then she looked up at me. "Stop."

Her joy and lust, the summer warmth and fire-smoke vanished, her emotions deadened. Millimeters stretched into an aching cavern of space.

"Don't," I said. "Don't do this."

My heart was splitting. The thunder and lightning no longer pulsed with desire. Instead, each beat, each bolt split and cracked my insides. I didn't want to hear it.

"We have to. We can't keep chasing this thing that can never be. We're not fated, Trey. You know that as well as I do, we can never be."

"I don't believe that," I said.

And I didn't. Not once did my faith waver. It was always her.

"It has to end. I can see it in your eyes."

I looked at the floor, desperate to stop her from making this decision.

"Cecilia... I wasn't going to tell you. But she found our encrypted mail. She's furious, threatened all kinds of things. But I don't understand why. Kato and Bo are seeing each other, and she's done nothing to prevent it. Why us? She's hiding something. I know it."

"Either way," she said.

Her words crushed. My chest tightened as I braced for what she'd say next.

"This... Us... We can't..."

She meant "love" each other. I wanted her to say it. To make it real. To tell me she loved me as much as I did her. If she'd said it, I'd have gone to The First Fallon there and then, fought her or died.

Perhaps Eden knew that and that's why the words never came. Instead, there was a thick pause filled with a fate that shouldn't be and a rage that hardened even the furthest reaches of my core. That was the moment I decided. As my soul hardened and the hope faded from my essence, I knew I couldn't continue the way things were. I couldn't attend Council meetings and play Fallons across from her. I couldn't go to balls and events knowing she would be there, so close and utterly unreachable. That would be torture. I didn't want her to see me with Eve any more than I wanted to watch her with who would inevitably turn out to be Victor.

The decision I made at that moment was wrong. But whether it was jealousy or rage or despair that made me do it, I don't recall.

"I know," I said. It hurt, my eyes stung. "But I don't want to be without you."

I pushed my lips onto hers. Harder, more urgent. I wanted to etch every part of our kiss into my memory. I needed to remember—to keep this moment. One last memory of perfection.

I kissed her with such intensity my heart threatened to break free from my ribs.

I whispered two words against her mouth. Two words that ruined everything.

"I'm sorry."

Tears streaked my cheeks as I reached for my essence. It rolled and flowed like water and oceans. And under it, the tug and pull of current and power.

The air rushed out of Eden's mouth. Her eyes shut as I tore out pieces of her. I pulled and pulled. Every late-night meeting, every Cog message, every brush of skin. I sucked and yanked until her memories pooled in the palm of my hand—giant and spinning particles of black and lilac warped and wobbled until they formed a ball.

When it was over, and I'd taken every memory of me from her, her face was slack. The hurt that carved frown lines into her skin and dulled her eyes had dissolved. That's what convinced me I'd done the right thing. She looked so peaceful, so free.

I leaned in, cheeks still wet, and whispered, "I love you Eden, in this lifetime and all the lifetimes to come."

Then I ran. Leaving her alone by the lake. I hid behind a tree big enough to shroud me in darkness and I watched as she opened her eyes and her world fell apart.

She stood for a moment, lost in confusion. She didn't know why she was at The Pink Lake. A sob ripped from her chest. I bit my lip to stop myself from calling out, running to her rescue and giving everything back.

She dragged herself toward Keepers school, tears and cries echoing through the Forest; her heart knew what had happened, but her mind had forgotten. That's the funny thing about Siren magic, we can convince the mind of anything, but the heart always knows the truth.

As she disappeared into the tree line and out of sight, the ball of her memories weighed heavy in my hand. A tangible reminder of the huge mistake I'd just made.

My chest was in agony. It was as though breaking her apart had broken me, too.

Long after she'd vanished from sight, her heart screamed so loud I could sense her pain. Like a bullet, it wound through the Forest and pierced my essence, my soul.

I'd fucked up. I was trying to help her, save her from the anguish of having to be with Victor whilst loving me. But I'd made a huge mistake. Instead of saving her, I'd made everything worse.

And what would happen if I ran after her, gave it all

back? What would she think? I couldn't bear it. So I did what I always did; I took my own pain away.

I turned around. A few feet away, just far enough she'd blended in with the shrubbery, Eve stood glaring at me.

"I—" I started, but she held her hand up.

"Was the kiss worth it?"

Her face was full of fire, the cool green of her irises burned hot, her jaw trembled.

Shit.

I couldn't answer. We both knew our Binding was a farce. There was no connection. Not like the books tell you there should be. I'd grown to love her, yes, but I was never going to yearn for her. I didn't need her. It didn't feel like a piece of my soul was missing when she went away.

She knew she felt it too, and yet, she'd committed to me, anyway. That's what made this so much worse.

"You wiped her, didn't you?" Eve said.

I looked away. I couldn't bear the pressure of her gaze anymore.

"Jesus, Trey. You cleaned her memories and still you're pining after her."

She screamed once and whipped her wand out, firing a thread of magic into the evening. It smacked into a tree and bark erupted from the trunk. Splinters shot into the air, they flew in a hundred directions, scattering to the ground.

"Why don't you ever look at me that way? I'm your Balancer for fuck's sake."

There was a beat. I swear even the night birds and insects fell quiet.

"But the truth is, I'm never going to be enough for you, am I?" Her wand arm fell to her side. "Because I'm not her."

I brought my eyes to meet hers. My mouth fell open, but she cut me off before I could respond.

"You know what? You should go tomorrow because everyone else apart from you realizes she's gone. She'll never be yours. And the sooner you accept that, the better. If I mean anything to you, you'll go to her fucking Potential ceremony and you'll watch the announcement, and then you'll erase her from your life."

I glanced at the ball still spinning in my hand. Eve was right. I had to go. Not because she wanted me to or because she wanted me to drop Eden. That would never happen. I had to go because I had to see The First Fallon, I needed to know if fate had truly given me to Eve and Eden to Victor or if this was just another of her games, another form of torture.

"Fine," I said. "I'll go."

She nodded at me and then hid her wand in her dress robe.

Then she slipped her hand in mine and we walked in silence back to the Council chambers for the evening.

EIGHT

'The truest love will always mark the soul.'

Balance proverb

December 2016

I'm still in Obex. I'm not sure how much longer the piece of
life inside me is going to last. From what Pest and Eve say,
the stench of "breather" still peels off me, though to a lesser
degree than when I first arrived. And understandably so.
I've been here for weeks. Far longer than I expected and
longer than Rozalyn initially implied was realistic. Whatever is still alive in me, there can't be much left. Which
means my time is running out and I need to push Rozalyn
to let me return. Thankfully, the army is almost ready.
Which means this may be one of my last entries. If it is,
thank you. Thank you for listening, for your lack of silent
judgment. I've decided I like this—the process of journaling,
of examining memories. I'm taking you back to Trutinor.
We're not done with each other. This has been so cathartic.

Despite having "memory" as my essence, I never realized how heavy memories were.

They have mass. I mean, it makes sense. When elderly Keepers lie on their deathbeds, it's not trivial memories that plague them. It's not the monotony of drinking herb tea each morning over the CogNews paper or their commute to work that fills their brains. It's the memories riddled with emotion that eat away at their last moments of happiness. But when a Siren unburdens them, everything changes. I think that's why I'm doing this. So that when I go back, I return free of memory pain.

Let me explain. I remember one elderly Keeper close to our family, a Sorcerer named Rafiq. He was lucky, he only had one memory, but it bore such weight on the man I'll never forget what happened when I released him from it.

He lay in his oak bed. The air was full of incense and fruit tea. His bedroom was a lethal weapon. How he hadn't broken his neck in there, I don't know. Old potion bottles littered the floor. Ancient books and grimoires smothered surfaces. I couldn't tell you what color the walls were. Parchment paper lined the walls, half-spells and passages scrawled in curly half-legible script.

His Balancer, Markus, had long since died. Loneliness etched into the lines and wrinkles that painted his skin. He was ready to meet Markus in Obex, that much was obvious, but something held him back. I had a feeling that's why he summoned me.

Rafiq's eyes fluttered open, his face relaxed a little, and he slumped further into bed.

"You came," he said.

"Of course."

He was the Sorcerer who prepared my father's Dust, but our families went back much further than that. His relationship with my family was much like Arden's to Eden's family.

"It's almost time," he said and tried to lift his frail hand.

I sat on the side of his bed and took his hand in mine. "I'm here, Rafiq. Tell me what you need."

He tilted his head away. Even years on, the memory pained him enough it brought tears to his eyes.

"I did something."

"Let it go, that's why I'm here."

"No," he said. "I don't want you to remove it. What I did... It's... I have to take it with me. But I want you to help me feel differently about it. It's the emotion that burdens me."

"Okay. Are you ready?"

His jaw stiffened. He took one haggard breath and then nodded. I touched his temple, where my fingertip met his skin an ocean-cool throb pulsed. It's a strange quirk of Sirenism that our power feels so much like the thing that's most dangerous to us. I'm sure it's because of how close we're related to Mermaids.

I pulled away. Where my finger moved through the air, a trail of green wispy smoke followed. I spun my fingers around until the green smoke formed a ball. Once it was complete, and no more memory appeared, I nudged the threads until smoky figures appeared.

Rafiq sat on the edge of a bed much as I am on his now.

But on his bed lay not an old man, but a small child. I stiffened and glanced at him. He turned away, his lips pressed flat.

Rafiq was a healing sorcerer. He worked closely with the Dryads. When traditional Dryad medicine had run its course, Rafiq would step in to see if there was anything he could do. It was a rotten job, but Rafiq had a reputation for saving lost causes. Magic, though, has its limits. Rafiq couldn't save them all. No one expected him to. That was a burden he placed on himself.

The boy squeezed Rafiq's hand and whispered thank you.

Rafiq cradled the boy's head and then helped him drink a small cup of liquid. My gut twisted. I'd seen enough memories to know where this was going. What he'd done.

Once the child lay still, Rafiq's shoulders rocked. He wiped his face and then two figures appeared. They spoke in soft tones. One figure dropped to their knees. The memory ended as Rafiq walked out of the room. He'd ended the child's life. The question was why.

The memory-ball continued to spin. I couldn't give it back yet. I was here to help him move on, which meant I had to shift something in the memory.

"Talk to me, Rafiq."

He was silent for a while, then he turned to me. "He was dying. What he had was incurable and he would get worse and his parents would have to watch their baby die in writhing agony…"

My mouth formed a small "o" shape as I realized what this was really about.

"How old was he when he died?" I asked.

"The boy?"

I shake my head. My father told me that Markus and Rafiq had adopted a child. This was long before I was born. But the child contracted a disease. There was nothing the Dryads could do. Rafiq tried everything, but still, he couldn't save his child.

"Markus didn't blame me, you know." He paused. The relief that had washed through him as I arrived vanished. His face aged as he spoke, his eyes drew down, wrinkles deepened. Memories are so powerful they can raise a man or ruin him. This one had ruined Rafiq.

"Markus told me time and time again, he knew how hard I'd tried to save our son."

"I'm so sorry," I said.

Rafiq shook, tears rolled down his cheeks, coursing their way over the wrinkled waves of his skin.

"It wasn't him dying that broke us. It was watching him wither. His strangled screams filling the night. The agony that tore through his limbs eating his muscles cell by cell. And no one could do a damn thing about it. We were totally helpless. I failed in the worst way possible."

"You didn't fail. There was nothing anyone could do. And the boy you helped to die, that was a mercy. You saved him from months of tort—"

"No," Rafiq said and grabbed my hand. "Don't you see? This wasn't about him. I didn't end his life to save him from the pain."

My eyes widened as I realized what he'd done.

"You saved his parents?"

"I was weak. They could have said goodbye. They could have had a few more months."

"No, Rafiq. You saved them and the boy from weeks of pain."

"I stole the most precious time a parent can have. It's unforgivable."

I squeezed his hand. "What's the last memory you have of your son?" I asked.

Rafiq's eyes welled once more, his brow creased. "I've tried to keep the memories of him as a toddler, of him playing with wands and herbs. But I'm plagued by his cries and little limbs bent and twisted in pain."

"Exactly. What you did was a gift. A kindness. That

boy's parents will live the rest of their lives with happy memories of their son. Instead of their dreams being filled with hollow screams and a mangled version of their child. They will dream of playtimes and laughter. They won't live the life of pain you did. If someone could have prevented you from having a life of pain, would you have let them?"

"I don't know. I would give anything for one more second with our son. But back then, I'd have done anything to take his pain away. I was too weak to take his life and stop the hurt."

"Rafiq..." I called. This time, my voice was melodic. The cool smoothness of compulsion licked the tones of my words.

"Yes, the boy's parent's mourned, but over time the loss faded into wonderful memories filled with love and not pain. What you did was a kindness. Look at your memory, see the good you did."

His face relaxed, the tension that had tightened his shoulders loosened. I threaded the memory back into his temple. He smiled once, then his eyes fluttered shut, and he died in my arms.

Do you see now? Do you see how powerful memories are? He went to his next life in peace.

As I sat on the end of his bed, I knew he'd lived so long because the memory had kept him here. It terrified me. I'd never forgiven myself for the boy I killed at my mother's Dusting. If I'd got to my death bed an old man, it would have plagued me like Rafiq's memory plagued him.

Like me, Rafiq's hands were stained with the blood of a young innocent. Children aren't meant to die. Their blood doesn't wash away no matter how much you scrub. It changes you. It changed him.

It's changed me too.

NINE

'I love you in this lifetime and all the lifetimes to come.'

Trey Luchelli and Eden East

Memories from December 2016

One thing I will miss about this place is the sky. There is something spectacular about Obex's perpetual twilight. The sky of the dead burns orange and pink. Brush strokes lick the clouds like molten paintings. If Rozalyn doesn't let me return to Trutinor, the sky is one thing I will take solace in.

So this is it. We're leaving Obex tomorrow. Eve pushed me over the edge. She made me fight her in the club; I won. And now a piece of her soul will forever be attached to mine.

I swear she antagonized me on purpose. This whole time, she was scheming and plotting. Everything orchestrated by her and Rozalyn. I'm not sure any of that even matters now. All that matters is that I leave and get home to Eden.

I've done what Rozalyn asked. She has her army. There's no reason to keep me here any longer.

I have one memory left I want to share. The memory of when everything went wrong. I should have stood up. Shouted, screamed, sabotaged. Done anything other than what I actually did. Which was stand there limp, pathetic. I watched instead of taking action. No more. Tomorrow everything changes.

It was the first of December. The day after Eden's birthday and that fateful night by the Pink Lake. Eden would have her Potential announced in the most anticipated Potential ceremony in a few decades. If the Council had listened, truly read the scriptures and allowed their essences to dig deep and connect with the threads of power in Trutinor, someone would have realized.

Eden was unsettled. She knew there was something off in the air. I only knew that because of Kato. And that is where we'll start.

Kato stormed into my room. We'd arrived in the Ancient Forest earlier that morning. Most of the students due to have their Potentials announced stayed on the school grounds and took the train here this morning. Kato and I had stayed in the Ancient Forest where most of the Fallon families were. I'd gotten in so late from sneaking out to see Eden at the Pink Lake, my eyes were stinging with exhaustion. There was a Council meeting first thing that morning. I forget now what it was about. Probably some drivel as usual.

The door to my office swung open and smashed against the wooden wall.

Kato raised his hand, index finger pointed up, other hand on his hip. My brother has always had drama threaded through his veins.

"What, dear brother, The Fuck?"

I took a deep breath, closed my CogTracker and leaned over it toward him.

"Number one, watch your mouth. Number two, I don't know what you're talking about."

I did, of course. But if I could avoid admitting what I'd done, then I would. Could I really trust my sixteen-year-old brother to hold a secret like that? Should I even? Was it fair to ask that of him? I never answered my question because Kato sashayed into the room, plonked himself in the chair in front of my desk, and kicked his feet onto my desk.

Which, I might add, I just as promptly shoved off.

"No, brother." He pointed an accusing finger at me. "You should watch your tone."

It took every ounce of strength not to slap it away. This was always the way between us. I spent fifty percent of my time trying to be the parent he needed and the other fifty suppressing the urge to punch my brother in the gut.

"And why is that?"

"Because you have committed quite the atrocity."

"Have I now? And what, precisely, have I done?"

Kato's eyes darkened. He leaned forward in the chair.

"Enough games. What did you do to Eden?"

"Like I said, I have no idea what you're talking about."

"Reaaaally?" His eyes narrowed. "Well, I look forward

to whatever bullshit concoction you come up with to explain this one away."

"Kato," I said, and slapped him upside the head, "I said watch your damn language."

He stood up, knocking the chair away.

"You know what, Trey. I'm kind of done. She's not in a good way this morning and has very little idea of who the hell you are, other than my brother. So you better spill before I drag her confused ass in here and tell her you stole her fucking memories."

Shit.

Kato always was the cleverer of us. I shifted in my seat, pushed my CogTracker around the desk. Eventually, I looked up.

"You're going to have to take Bo's memories too," Kato barked.

"Not a chance. Don't you think I've done enough damage?"

"Well, I can't do it, she's about to be my Potential. And how the hell are you going to get Bo to toe the line if you don't? If you think for a second Bo won't tell Eden..." Kato said. "Jesus, Trey. Why spend all those nights sneaking out to see her? Why allow yourself to fall for her?"

I cocked my head at him. I thought I'd kept those meetings secret. He rolled his eyes as if mocking my ignorance. Of course, he knew. There was very little Kato didn't know, even at his young age.

"What did you expect me to do? Yes, I am completely and utterly in love with Eden. But I'm already Bound for Balancesake. It was never going to end well. It's not like we'd magically become Potentials today. Why live with the hurt?"

"So you stole her memories?"

"What would you have had me do?"

"How about give her the fucking choice? And I thought you were the older one. Jesus, Trey. You have royally fucked this one up."

"LANGUAGE."

"No," he snapped, and stood up. A slender finger pointed right at me. "You don't get to be the adult in this conversation. You made a mistake. Now give back her memories before I make you give them back."

"This is not up for debate."

"So what? You expect me and Bo to harbor your secret like some filthy smugglers?"

"View it as you wish, Kato. But keep it, you must."

His mouth pinched tight. He kicked the table leg and stood up, opening his arms at me, gesticulating.

"And when Eden finds out I knew? What then?"

I shook my head and ran my hand through my hair. We didn't have time for this. I didn't want to explain myself to a sixteen-year-old, least of all my brother.

I rounded on him. "She won't find out. And this conversation is done. Either you both do as you're told and stay quiet, or you're going to step up and take your girlfriend's memories. But this secret *is* being kept, Kato. I swear to Balance—" the vault rumbled. Just enough, Imbalance shivered over my vision. A haze of red Kato was familiar with.

He stepped back. A furrow between his eyes, then held up his hands, "Fine. You win, Trey. But don't expect me to mop your tears when this goes wrong. And I assure you, it will."

He backed out of the office, his jaw flexed in time with his footsteps.

He didn't speak to me for the rest of the day. Even when I brought him his Potential ceremony gift. He took it, glared at me and marched off with Beatrice, whose blank expression told me he'd done as I'd asked.

After he left the office, I flipped my palm open and pulled up Eden's memory ball.

Had I done the right thing? Was this all a horrible mistake?

I left and made my way to the ceremony hall. I slid my fingers over the ornate metal handle and pressed down. It creaked, my insides tingled. Everything about that day was wrong. I threw a quick glance over my shoulder. It would piss Eve off that I'd watched the ceremony without her. But I needed this time alone. I had to say goodbye to Eden in my own way. And perhaps part of me also wanted to make sure she was okay. I pushed the door to the viewing balcony open and slipped inside.

The box was lush, made of navy velvets and studded with gold buttons, much like the Chesterfield furniture in the South. Midnight blue drapes, as soft as the clouds, hung from each side of the box. The main auditorium seating was usually enough seating for the Potential ceremonies. Which is how I knew I'd be alone up here. I was at least twenty feet higher than the stage. Enough to not be noticed. But even so, I stayed in the shadows, lost inside the curtain's ruffles.

The First Fallon stepped on stage, her ghostly figure floated. Such a strange vision she was, angelic and serene and yet when alone, she was a violent bitch. She scanned the crowd, her eyes flicked for the briefest moment up to the balcony stall. I flinched and shuffled further into the curtains. When I looked back at her, she was smiling at the audience and I was certain she hadn't spotted me.

The ceremony started, a stream of students filed on and off stage. The Balance Scriptures—six cogs filled with colored smoke lay before The First Fallon. She would pull strands of smoke and gesticulate wildly as she pronounced Potential pairings.

It was all a farce, a sordid show, some twisted game to keep the masses controlled.

Kato's name was called. He walked on stage, his eyes skirted up to the balcony. The First Fallon may not have caught me, but Kato definitely knew where I was. His face was hard, a scowl pinched his lips. He didn't stare at the balcony long. This was a game, and he had a part to play. He bowed to The First Fallon and stood dutifully by her side while she picked another thread from the scriptures.

He fidgeted, but everyone knew whose name was going to be called. I remember his expression when the thread's color materialized. It was black, of course. His scrunched-up brow relaxed instantly, even before Beatrice's name was said.

The words drifted off The First Fallon's lips, Kato's face erupted, giant smiles and enormous eyes. But I also remember how I felt at that moment. My chest flared hot. A sharp stab pummeled my fist. I looked at the wall. My hand was inside it. I pulled my hand out. I'd cut it in two places, the knuckles swollen. As I write this, I can almost taste bile in my mouth from back then.

I'm not proud.

But can you really blame me? My brother was getting everything he ever wanted. His Potential was the girl he'd loved from the first moment he saw her. I wanted that. Everyone does.

I was happy for him, of course. But there was a piece of me that needed to hurt because I would never feel the unadulterated happiness painting joy lines into his expression.

Beatrice slipped her hand into Kato's and they walked

offstage together. I pulled on my essence, and muted the pain enough to stop the bleeding, but not enough to eradicate the dull throb that was keeping me grounded.

A few more Keepers were called, and then—

"Fallon Eden East?" The First Fallon said.

Eden sloped on stage, reluctance written in the slant of her shoulders. Her eyes were skittish, jumping from the scriptures to The First Fallon and roving over the stage. They were puffy, too. Red-rimmed, despite the makeup I'm sure Beatrice helped her put on.

I slid to the front of the balcony, leaning over as if that might somehow get me close enough to stop Cecilia. I knew it was foolish, but every cell in my body ached with the wrongness of what was happening. Back then, The First Fallon still had her claws in me. She held too much power over me. I'd only just escaped her experiments. I didn't have it in me to fight for Eden, too. It was cowardly.

My fingers gripped the balcony's edge, knuckles white like snow-capped mountain peaks. The door creaked. I couldn't bring myself to look behind me. I didn't need to either. As soon as it inched open, the reek of berries and burned wood drifted in, mottled with sour cherry. It was a cloying mix of desperation and desire that followed Evelyn. My stomach hardened. I wanted to see this on my own. I needed the time by myself to process. She knew that deep down. Which is exactly why she couldn't let me have it.

Eve didn't move any closer. She stayed behind me, silent, observing. The atmosphere was thick, filled with all the things we should admit and couldn't, or maybe didn't want to.

This wasn't about Eve. She would get enough of me soon enough. I concentrated on Eden, the stage. She took a deep, shuddering breath and shut her eyes. I leaned a little further forward. Every part of me wanted to wrap my arms around her. To smother her in reassurance. To slide my hand in hers and convince her it was going to be all right. But I didn't. I couldn't.

I stayed put. My eyes stung, my throat was hard and tight. Eden might have shut her eyes, but I couldn't tear mine away. My ears filled with the roar of blood. I couldn't hear shit. But I could lip read. I knew what was coming.

"Fallon Victor Dark," The First Fallon said. As she said Victor's name, her eyes hardened. She glanced up at my balcony box. Her gaze met mine for one long, potent pause. This time, there was no mistaking it. She looked right at me. Her eyes glittered, her pale lips curled into a snarl.

Eden's mouth dropped, her shoulders slanted forward, and a single word rippled out on her breath. "No."

The hot well of poison and lava frothed inside me. I wanted to kill Victor. I wanted to climb on stage and rip the little wolf's heart out.

As Victor swaggered on stage, my fingers bit into the wood. The sneer curling his lips read, "I won."

My vision deepened, the maroon of Imbalance hazed my sight. I was going to lose control. I was going to tear the place down and kill everyone. All it would take was a flick of my wrist and I'd infect the auditorium. I'd push a slow acute pain through their spinal cords. A delicious mix of searing nerves and the ice-cold prickle of horror.

Eve's hand found mine, and it snapped my focus back to the present. Her fingers slotted into the grooves over mine. My hand reacted automatically, shunting and snapping off the wooden top rail. I stepped back from the edge and dropped the redundant wood. I grabbed her wrist.

"Whatever you do to me, I'll take it," she said. "No

matter how much you hurt me, I won't leave. I'm here for you, Trey, whether you like it or not."

"Why? You don't want this any more than I do." My voice was bitter, detached. Her lips pressed together as her eyes scanned my face. She reached for me with her free hand. This made me loosen my grip on her arm.

"I may have had no choice when I was sent here to you. But that doesn't make me powerless. It doesn't make you powerless, either."

I frowned at her.

"I choose to be here for you. I choose you."

And I choose Eden.

I closed my eyes and when I opened them again, I glanced down at the stage. Eden was walking off, her hand in Victor's. My jaw flexed, my teeth ground over each other. Even from as high as I was, the tremors making her hands shake were obvious.

I reached for my essence, the tingle of power threaded through my body. I shut everything off. Turned the tap tight on my emotions. I didn't want to deal with any of it.

"Trey?" Eve said. "Will you choose me too?"

I didn't answer. I couldn't.

There was a war raging beneath my skin. I couldn't give myself to Evelyn when my heart was consumed by Eden. I didn't care if she was fated to another. Every ounce of my soul knew it was a lie.

So I shut my eyes, breathed deep and buried every emotion but Eden. I flattened the sharp throb in my chest, the ache that seemed to inhabit every cell even though I couldn't quite touch it. I buried everything but her.

Eden stepped down the stage stairs and, for a brief second, looked up. Our eyes met. She frowned, but it was a blank stare. Empty of memories and emotion. Empty because I stole them. My fingers flexed instinctively, calling the threads of her memories into my palm. I snapped my hand shut. Not while Evelyn was with me. Those memories were mine. Eve might have me, but she wouldn't have that.

Eden's blank stare didn't last long. She turned back to Victor and they disappeared out of sight.

Even though I'd removed all my emotions, something inside me cracked and fell away. If I'd left my emotions on, I know I'd have collapsed. But I was numb and empty.

"She's gone. It's over," Eve said.

Something twitched inside me, but I could no longer tell if it was rage, disappointment or something else.

"You're never going to be together," she said. "Are you ready to let go of this childish crush and choose me?"

My teeth snapped shut. I knew it was over. That didn't mean I wanted her reminder. Especially when her eyes glittered with the same look as The First Fallon's. I glared at her, my body rigid with suppression. She was lucky I'd switched everything off.

Even as I sit here writing this years on, I know if I'd turned my emotions back on, I'd have killed her. Her brazen dismissal of Eden and my feelings made my veins burn.

That was the only moment I've ever hated Eve. I hated her for everything she wasn't. For everything she represented. But more than any of that, I hated her for my weakness. I blamed her.

"Are you going to make a life with me?" she said.

I glanced down. In my palm, the tickle of Eden's memory ball spiraled and hissed.

"Yes." I squeezed her memories away, pushed them deep insides myself. When I knew they were safe, I looked up at her. "Yes, I am."

As certain as I was that Eden should have been my

Balancer, I was convinced that Evelyn knew every word I said was a lie. I'd never give up the fight to get Eden back. My heart is, was, and always will be hers.

It was at that moment, as I stared over the broken balcony, at the space Eden had filled moments ago, that I swore to myself. I did not know how I'd prevent it, but Eden would not be Bound to Victor. It was wrong. My Binding to Eve was wrong. We both knew it, and yet we played along with the charade, anyway. All to appease The First Fallon.

I had work to do. I wasn't losing Eden a second time. Not when I knew I loved her. Not when I knew my Binding to Eve was wrong. The fact no one had ever corrected a Binding didn't mean shit to me. I was resolute. This farce had to end.

Right there, on the balcony, as I held Eve's hand and stared into her green eyes, I knew everything we'd share would be a lie. I'd have to take what happiness I could and try to make a semblance of a life with her, for both our sakes.

I was going to get Eden back no matter the cost, because I'd love her in this lifetime and all the lifetimes to come.

Do you love juicy character gossip…?

Dive into the exclusive short story, only available to download here:

sachablack.co.uk/keepersbonus

This short story is set during the summer after *Keepers*, you'll find out:

- Insider secrets from the biggest Keepers party of the summer.
- What Eden and Trey's relationship was like after they were Bound but before the events of *Victor*.
- What Bo and Kato were like after his betrayal.

Get it now.

 instagram.com/sachablackauthor

 facebook.com/sachablackauthor

Get the complete series now...

The Eden East Novels:

- Book 1 - Keepers
- Book 2 - Victor
- Book 3 - Trey
- Book 4 - Sirens (a short bonus novella set in Obex)

Printed in Great Britain
by Amazon